C000021141

For my mother,
Gwen Niehaus

British Library Cataloguing in Publication Data
Bouma, Paddy
Bertie visits granny
I. Title
823[J]   PZ7
ISBN 0-370-31044-6

Copyright © Paddy Bouma 1987
Photoset by Rowland Phototypesetting Ltd
Bury St Edmunds, Suffolk
Printed in Great Britain for
The Bodley Head Ltd
32 Bedford Square, London WC1B 3EL
by W. S. Cowell Ltd,
Ipswich, Suffolk
First published 1987

Bertie
Visits Granny

Paddy Bouma

The Bodley Head
London

Bertie the hippo lived on Thomas's bed.
He was warm and cuddly, and
comfortable to sleep on. He was
Thomas's favourite toy.

One day Thomas took Bertie along to
visit Granny at her shop.

"You must be hungry, Thomas," said
Granny. Thomas put Bertie down on the
floor, while he ate a packet of jellybeans,
a slice of chocolate cake, some crisps
and a banana.

The sight of all this food made Bertie
feel hungry, too. Horatio the bulldog's
bowl was on the floor. Bertie edged
closer to it . . .

Horatio gave a menacing growl.

"Bad dog," said Granny. "Leave poor Bertie alone." And she turned Horatio out on to the pavement.

Granny put Bertie up on a washstand out of harm's way.

Moses the cat had his saucer of milk up there. Bertie sniffed at it.

Moses's hair stood on end and he spat
at Bertie. The saucer crashed to the
floor.

"Moses, how could you be so clumsy?"
said Granny.

She put Moses out into the yard.

Bertie was moved to an oak dresser. Double-O-Seven the parrot had his cage up there. Bertie looked hard at Double-O-Seven's beak and decided that he did not fancy birdseed.

Little Gideon wandered by with an ice-cream cone. Bertie leaned over and took a lick.

Gideon burst into tears.

"Double-O-Seven, you bad bird!" said Granny. "To scare poor Gideon like that!" And she put Double-O-Seven into his cage.

Thomas said that he thought it was time to take Bertie home.

"Bertie, you were *awful*," said
Thomas. "I'm ashamed of you."
But Bertie did not reply. He was too
busy nosing in Thomas's pocket for the
last of the jellybeans.